# PUFFIN BITES

# Ginger

## Christobel Mattingley

### Illustrated by Margaret Power

PUFFIN BOOKS

For another Hugo and Harriet,
and their mother and father

PUFFIN BOOKS

Published by the Penguin Group
Penguin Books Ltd, 27 Wrights Lane, London W8 5TZ, England
Penguin Putnam Inc., 375 Hudson Street, New York, New York 10014, USA
Penguin Books Australia Ltd, Ringwood, Victoria, Australia
Penguin Books Canada Ltd, 10 Alcorn Avenue, Toronto, Ontario,
Canada M4V 3B2
Penguin Books (NZ) Ltd, Private Bag 102902, NSMC,
Auckland, New Zealand

On the worldwide web at: www.penguin.com

Penguin Books Ltd, Registered Offices: Harmondsworth,
Middlesex, England

First published in Australia by Penguin Books Australia Ltd, 1997
Published in Puffin Books, 2000

1 3 5 7 9 10 8 6 4 2

Made and printed in Australia by Australian Print Group,
Maryborough, Victoria
Series designed by Ruth Grüner

British Library Cataloguing in Publication Data
A CIP catalogue record for this book is available from the British Library

ISBN 0-141-30948-2

0141 309 482 5201

# One

Hugo adored Ginger.

Ginger was soft and snuggly.
Ginger was clever and cuddly.
Ginger was furry and friendly
and fun.

Hugo knew Ginger was the
best rabbit in the world.

Snowdrop was white as
meringue and pretty as a rose.
Tomboy was black as licorice and
bold as a crow. Harriet thought
her rabbits were the best in
the world.

The children's mother loved all the rabbits. And she loved the other animals too, just as much as Hugo and Harriet did – Murphy the labrador and Lulu the poodle, Martha the tortoiseshell and Samuel the tabby.

But the children's father didn't have much time for animals. He didn't like dog hairs on his clothes or dog lick on his hands. And he simply abominated dog droppings on his lawn.

Cats made him sneeze. And as for rabbits – if one of them so much as nibbled a pansy or nipped a parsley sprig, he would frown and rumble.

But Hugo loved to let them out of their hutch to frisk on the grass and frolic through the bushes. So he spent hours in the garden keeping watch on the rabbits.

He loved to watch Ginger

scamper across the lawn and

hide behind a clump of daisies.

He loved to listen to his sharp
little teeth cropping the clover
and munching the thistles.

He loved to watch the ginger whiskers twitch, the pink nose sniff, the long silky ears quiver, alert and listening. Ginger – so alive and so inquisitive. Ginger the adventurer.

When the family went to the country for the weekend, Martha and Samuel stayed at home. 'Cats like home best, and the neighbours will look after them,' the children's mother said. 'But dogs need exercise, so we must take Murphy and Lulu. And Hugo and Harriet will fret without the rabbits,' she told their father. 'So we must take Ginger, Snowdrop and Tomboy.'

'Plenty of rabbits in the country,' their father growled.

'But not like Ginger, Dad!' Hugo said.

'*Please,* Dad,' Harriet pleaded.

'All right then,' their father

grumbled, heaving the hutch into the station wagon. Murphy and Lulu bounded into the back seat and he sighed at the thought of vacuuming up the dog hairs again.

# Two

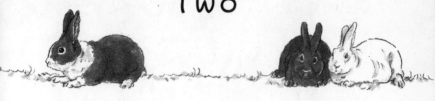

All the way to the farm, Ginger snuggled warm and cosy in Hugo's arms. Ginger's nose and whiskers twitched. But his ears lay still against Hugo's chest. Hugo wondered if Ginger could hear his heart beating, just as he

could feel Ginger's through his soft red-gold fur.

Murphy and Lulu pranced and wagged their tails. They stuck their heads out of the windows, barking at windmills and trains. When the children's father exclaimed, 'We're like a travelling circus!' Hugo and Harriet laughed and clapped.

In the country all the family was happy.

Snowdrop and Tomboy played
on the grass under the old apple
trees. Harriet puffed all the
dandelion clocks she could find.

Ginger went exploring, but Murphy
and Lulu kept a watchful eye on
him.

Hugo's mother swung in a
hammock and read a book.

Even the children's father was
cheerful. He helped Hugo build
a treehouse.

Just as the trees were turning

black against an orange sky,

Hugo hammered the last nail into the treehouse.

'Bathtime!' their mother said.

Harriet hustled Ginger, Snowdrop and Tomboy into their hutch. Hugo followed his mother into the kitchen. He was hungry. He began scrubbing carrots and potatoes.

'I'll feed the rabbits,' their father offered. Harriet opened her eyes wide at her mother.

Everyone looked surprised as he took the bowl of vegetable scraps from the kitchen sink. He never fed the rabbits as a rule. He walked out humming into the dark, while their mother hustled Hugo and Harriet into the bath.

# Three

Later, from his bed by the
window, Hugo counted stars. A
willie wagtail called in the apple
trees and at the farm down the
road, dogs barked. Murphy
snored at the foot of Hugo's bed

and Lulu whimpered in her sleep beside Harriet.

Hugo thought of Ginger snug in the hutch with Snowdrop and Tomboy, sniffing grassy smells, dreaming dandelion dreams.

Hugo woke with the sound of kookaburras and jumped out of bed. He ran outside, across the grass to the rabbit hutch.

The door was open . . .

Cowering in a corner was Snowdrop. Trembling and terrified. But of Ginger and Tomboy there was no trace . . .

'Harriet! Mum! Dad!' Hugo shouted. 'Ginger! Oh Ginger!' He began to run . . .

Through the gate . . . Across
the paddock . . . A tuft of black
fur on a dry thistle. 'Tomboy!'
A splash of blood on a stone.
'Ginger! Oh Ginger!'

His dad caught up with him
just as he came upon their
bodies. Tossed aside like old
socks. A night's sport for the farm
dogs . . . Hugo sobbed as he
picked up Ginger.

His dad picked up Tomboy. 'I'm

sorry, Hugo,' he said gruffly. 'I'm really sorry. I couldn't have fixed the latch properly in the dark. Though I thought I did.' They walked back slowly, without another word. Hugo did not feel the prickles in his feet. He could only feel the pain in his heart. And Ginger cold and stiff in the cradle of his arms.

He laid Ginger gently in the treehouse and fetched a spade.

He lined the hole
his father dug with
autumn-gold apple
leaves and laid
Ginger and Tomboy
in it.

Hugo hid his face against his father.

'It wasn't your fault, Dad. I know that. But I'll miss him. Terribly. Ginger was the best rabbit in the world. There'll never be another rabbit like Ginger.'

They went inside.

# Four

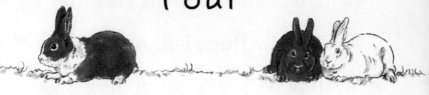

Harriet was setting the table
for breakfast. Their mother was
making coffee. Hugo loved the
smell of coffee, but this morning
it made him feel sick. He rushed
for the bathroom.

When he came back, his dad

was standing in the middle of the kitchen, his big strong hands hanging helpless at his side. He looked how Hugo felt. As if all the stuffing had gone out of him. Like the scarecrow Hugo and Harriet had made.

Their mother looked up from the coffee grinder. She looked from their father to Hugo. 'What's the matter?'

Hugo's throat closed up. The

words refused to come.

His father said in a slow tight voice, 'I couldn't have fixed the latch properly last night. The farm dogs got the rabbits.'

Harriet's eyes went wide and dark. She gave a little moan. Their mother dropped a mug.

Hugo grabbed Harriet's arm. 'They didn't get Snowdrop.'

Harriet pulled away and rushed outside. Hugo knew where

she was going. Knew what she was feeling. He let her go. She didn't need anyone. Yet.

His mother put her arms around his father. 'Oh, John,' she said. 'Oh, John! How awful for you.'

And me, Hugo thought. What about me? He knelt to pick up the pieces of the broken mug. The floor was hard and cold. Then he felt his mother's arms around him, soft and warm. He smelled her smell and the hot tears came. Through his sobs he could hear his father poking the fire, poking it, poking it, slamming the stove door, thumping outside to the woodbox.

'Dad didn't mean to,' he heard his mother saying.

'I know,' he mumbled and brushed the tears from his eyes.

He looked up. Harriet was

standing there. Standing there

with Snowdrop in her arms.

'Want to have a hold? She can be half yours now.'

She crouched down beside him and passed Snowdrop into his empty arms. His arms that ached for Ginger. Snowdrop was still shivering. He stroked her. Stroked her soft white fur, as white as meringue. Felt her slowly growing calm and warm.

Their father was holding Harriet. Now she was shivering,

sobbing. Her father was stroking her hair, 'I'm sorry, kids. I'm truly sorry.'

'We know, Dad. We know you are. We do know,' Hugo said. And Harriet nodded, her face still pressed against their father.

Their mother said. 'The fire's just right now for toast. And there's the strawberry jam we made in the summer.'

Hugo remembered helping to

pick the strawberries. With Ginger hopping along beside him, nipping the odd blossom. Now the strawberries were floating like clots in the bright jam. Red like congealing blood. He pushed Snowdrop back onto Harriet and ran outside.

# Five

Murphy and Lulu bounced up.
Hugo pushed them away. 'You
stupid fat things! What's the use
of you as watchdogs?' He went
down to the hutch and began
dragging it away. Away to a fresh
place where the grass had not

been trodden by the farm dogs.
He grabbed some thistles from
the strawberry patch and put
them ready. For Snowdrop.

Presently everyone came outside. His father was dressed. So were his mother and Harriet. Only Hugo was still in his pyjamas. His bloodstained pyjamas.

'There's still hot water if you want a shower,' his mother said.

Hugo knew that his father must have stoked up the fire specially. Usually they let it die down on the morning of the day they were leaving to go back to town.

'Let's finish burying Ginger and Tomboy,' Hugo said.

Carefully he picked golden leaves to cover Ginger. Harriet chose red ones for Tomboy. Gently their father spaded the soil back into the hole. Their mother covered the raw brown mound with dewy dandelions.

Their father went back to the

shed with the spade and came out with the saw. When he started cutting into one of the apple trees, their mother protested. 'It's too early, John, to be pruning. The leaves haven't finished falling.'

'Can't help that,' their father said. 'I've got to do it.'

All morning their father sawed and cut at the old apple trees. All morning their mother yanked

and tugged at the weeds. Hugo
helped and Harriet helped. The pile
of logs grew. The pile of weeds grew.

Hugo wheeled barrow-loads of
mossy old logs to the wood shed
without speaking.

He hated to see the trees
all cut because of Ginger.
All punished because of the
farm dogs. All cut and punished

because in the
dark his father
had not closed the
latch properly.

'I should have done this years ago,' his father said. 'Next year we'll get our best crop of apples ever. You'll see. And apple wood's great for burning. Smells beautiful.'

Hugo wheeled barrow-loads of juicy weeds to the compost heap. Fat milky thistles, lush long grass that Ginger and Tomboy would have munched so happily, but which was far too much for Snowdrop alone.

The heap was high and green. 'We'll put some soil over it,' his mother said. 'By spring it will be all rotted down and we can plant pumpkins in it.'

Hugo looked at the little mound under the apple tree. But he couldn't let himself think about that.

# Six

At lunchtime he ate some bread,
but he pushed away the salad
bowl. He couldn't eat lettuce. He
couldn't eat carrots. Not today.

It was quiet in the car going
home. Even Murphy and Lulu
were quiet. Harriet gave

Snowdrop to Hugo to nurse. And after a while Hugo gave her back. He knew Harriet was hurting too.

When they were nearly home, their father cleared his throat and said, 'I tell you what, kids. Tomorrow I'll leave the office early and we'll go to the pet shop. And I'll buy you each a rabbit.'

'No, Dad. No!' Hugo was shocked at the sound of his own voice. High and loud, yet sort of strangled. He looked at Harriet. There were tears on her eyelashes. 'I mean, Harriet might like another rabbit. But don't get one for me.'

Harriet shook her head and the tears dropped into Snowdrop's fur where they glittered like diamonds on a princess. 'Thank you, Dad,' she said. 'But Hugo and I like Snowdrop best.'

Lulu laid her head on Hugo's

knee and Murphy leaned against his legs. He stroked them both and noticed that his mother was stroking his father's arm.

Next day at school Hugo's teacher told the class to write about the worst thing that had happened on the weekend. Hugo opened his journal. He chose his best pen and wrote in his best writing. *'Ginger died.'*

Usually he filled a page. Often

he had to go over onto the next

because there was so much to say.

But now the page stared up at

him blankly. What else was there to say?

The teacher looked over his shoulder. 'You're slow getting started today, Hugo.' Then she read the two words he had written. She patted his shoulder. 'Perhaps another day, later on, you can write about Ginger, what was special about him, why you loved him. I feel I know him already from what you've written other times.'

# Seven

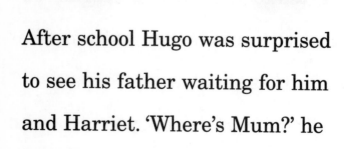

After school Hugo was surprised to see his father waiting for him and Harriet. 'Where's Mum?' he asked.

'Someone came to see her,' his father said.

'Where's the car?'

'I thought we'd walk.'

Hugo looked at his father suspiciously. 'Not to the pet shop,' he said. 'I don't want another rabbit,' and he could hear his voice rising as Harriet came up with a friend.

'Dad, Laura's asked me home to play. Can I go, please?'

Their father nodded and Harriet walked off arm in arm with her friend.

'I thought we could go through
the park,' Hugo's dad said.

'You can show me how you go on the fitness trail. We could do it together. But you'll be better than I am.'

Every afternoon that week Hugo's dad came to school. Every afternoon Harriet went off with her friend, and Hugo and his dad walked home through the park. Hugo was better on the balancing beam and the overhead ladder and the rings. But his dad improved, until by Friday he was nearly as good.

On Saturday his dad took him to the football. And on Sunday they went fishing.

Harriet was hanging round the gate when they drove home. 'You've been so long. I thought you were never coming.' She was hopping up and down with excitement. 'Come on! I've got something to show you! A surprise!' She led the way to the rabbit hutch. 'Look!'

Snowdrop had made a nest in the farthest corner and in it were three baby rabbits – one white, one black and one ginger.

'You can have whichever one you like, Hugo,' Harriet said. 'As long as it's not the white one or the black one.' She grinned at him.

And Hugo grinned back.

On Monday when his teacher asked the class to write about the best thing that had happened on the weekend, Hugo chose his best pen and wrote in his best writing, *'Ginger is a father!'*

## From Christobel Mattingley

When I was seven, my parents gave me two rabbits for Christmas. One was black, the other white. There was a heatwave and poor little Magic died. I was very sad, but my parents and sister helped me give her a flowery funeral.

When I heard how Hugo and Harriet lost their rabbits, I knew just how they felt, and I sat up late that night, beginning to write *Ginger*.

## From Margaret Power

When I was small and we lived in the country, my brothers had rabbits, but I was always bringing home stray cats.

One day, when I was about five, I was walking along our country lane. A man came along with an armful of kittens. 'Are these yours?' he asked. 'Oh yes!' I said, and took them home with great tenderness. It was lucky my mother liked them too.

# Hungry for more?

# Have a Bite!

Aussie Bites

The Too-Tight Tutu

Illustrated by
Cathy Wilcox

Sherryl Clark

Merry dreams of being
a ballerina. And nothing
is going to stop her . . .

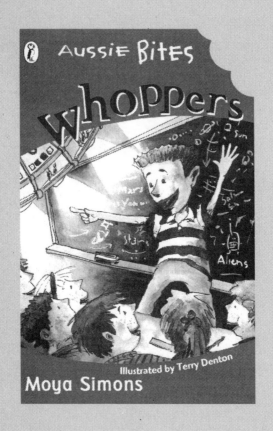

Mark swears he's a Martian.

But is he telling the truth?